For my father.

I. Guana and I thank Red, whose
lizards are truly an inspiration.

©1995 by Nina Laden.
All rights reserved.

Book design by Cathleen O'Brien.
Typeset in Old Typewriter Regular and Alternate.
The illustrations in this books were rendered in pastels.
Printed in Hong Kong

Library of Congress Cataloging-in-Publication Data
Laden, Nina.
Private I. Guana : the case of the missing chameleon
/ by Nina Laden.
p.   cm.
Summary : Private I. Guana is hired to
search the forest for Leon, a missing chameleon.
ISBN: 0-8118-0940-4
1. Iguanas-Fiction.   2. Chameleons-Fiction.
3. Mystery and detective stories.
4. Humorous stories.   I. Title.
PZ7.L13735Pr   1995
Fic -dc20   95-2828   CIP   AC

Distributed in Canada by Raincoast Books
8680 Cambie Street, Vancouver, B.C. V6P 6M9

10 9 8 7 6 5 4 3 2 1

Chronicle Books
275 Fifth Street, San Francisco, California 94103

PRIVATE I. GUANA

The
Case
of the
Missing
Chameleon

by Nina Laden

Chronicle Books · San Francisco

7⁵⁰

I was sitting at my desk
when I got the call. "Private
I. Guana here," I said. "Yes,
I can find missing lizards. A
chameleon? Well . . . okay.
Why don't you come over to my
office. And bring a photo."
As I hung up, I wondered if
I should have said okay.
Chameleons are hard to find.
But she sounded upset. I guess
I'm a sucker for a lizard in
distress.

"**You** can call me Liz," she said as she made herself comfortable in my office. "Here is a recent snapshot of Leon. He didn't come home for dinner one night last week. I had made his favorite, cricket stew . . . I haven't seen him since. He was acting a little strange, changing colors every minute. He's always been the stay-at-home type, and well, frankly . . . boring. I'm afraid he could be in trouble." I puffed myself up and said, "Now, don't you worry, Liz. If I can't find Leon, no one can. By the way," I asked, "what color was he when you last saw him?"

Quickly I made a pile of posters of Leon, the missing chameleon. Not knowing what color he was, I figured I'd color each poster differently. Too bad Leon didn't have a scar, or a tattoo. Then I set out to hang them up wherever I could. I stopped first to check in with Officer Croaker, the bullfrog chief of police. Officer Croaker, who had a habit of jumping to conclusions, said, "A missing chameleon? That's a waste of time. Probably pretending to be a rock." I said, "Thanks for your help, Officer. Maybe I'll go talk to some boulders."

SO I hit the dirt to see what I could dig up. I plastered the forest with posters. I went over fields, under rocks, and up trees. I talked to turtles, lizards, snakes, frogs, toads, and a couple of skinks. It was getting dark. My feet were tired, my tongue was tied, and I had no clues, no tales, no trails, no Leon. Maybe this chameleon had really disappeared for good. But maybe I just wasn't looking in the right place.

I decided to head
home and start again in the
morning. On the way, I saw a
firefly-like glow in the distance
by the swamp. I had forgotten
all about The Lizard Lounge.
It was kind of a slimy place,
where only the most cold-blooded
reptiles hung out. My head
was telling me not to go there.
But my stomach said, "Boy, I
sure could go for some of
those greasy fried grasshoppers
and a tall cold drink." So I
put my stomach in charge and
followed it.

The Lizard Lounge was buzzing with activity. I scoped out the place, making sure not to ruffle any feathers or step on any tails. I made my way to the back and sat at a table where I could keep an eye on things. The menu was my first order of business. I noticed that the special this week was cricket stew. "It's probably just a coincidence," I thought to myself.